BLOSSOMS

STORIES, ARTICLES, & PHOTOGRAPHS

BY SANDRA GRACE

Sandra Fram

Author & Editor
Sandra Grace

Website
wingsinthestorm.ca

Stock Photos
Butterflies & Raindrops; Reflections of a Father; Son of the Father; Mother

All Other Photos
Sandra Grace

First Edition

Published by Sandra Fram

BLOSSOMS

Butterflies & Raindrops

Interspersed throughout our lives, in the humdrum and the storms, are flashes of beauty that interrupt our scurry and cares—a word; a smile; the glories of nature. Sometimes with grandeur, they astound. Sometimes with soft whispers, they warm our hearts.

It was during a time of difficulty for me that I witnessed two such unforgettable displays. They were moments touched by God because I'm His, and He waits for me when I'm far from Him.

The afternoon was warm and sunny as I trudged alone along the road. I forced myself, each day, to make this march whether I felt like it or not. I was just about to my turning point when it happened. I didn't even notice them till I was in their midst.

Suddenly, they were there...

Exquisite yellow butterflies. There must have been eight or ten. They came up from the ground in a flutter, dancing. Delicate and elegant. They circled and swirled around me—my legs; my torso; my arms; my head. A kaleidoscope. A pageant. They took their time like they were playing. Laughing...pulling me into their joy.

They'd come there to meet me; they'd waited for me. To put light in my heart, a smile on my lips, and strength in my step. I stood transfixed, an undeserving guest at the centre of their celebration. It was one moment of indescribable beauty when time paused to give adoration.

Then they were gone.

The second event was on another walk. This day had a mystical aura—no breeze, no rustle of leaves. All was silent and still. Like I was the only one on earth. The clouded sky was bright, not like the usual dismal grey of an overcast day in New Brunswick.

It came without warning—there was no wind, no darkening skies. Just...

Rain.

Rain is cold in New Brunswick; it drives the heat away. But not this time. This rain fell straight down in gentle drops, fragrant and clean. It was not heavy or fierce but a quiet patter that tapped the leaves. Light; rhythmic; melodic. Warm beads against my skin. Warm air clung to the earth, refusing to flee. Thick forest and lush vegetation swelled to the moisture and drank it in. Showers sang; they soothed. Fresh and new and free.

Glorious!

These moments weren't just for me. They were God's expression of His majesty like He flings out every day across the universe. He is God. All nature sings His praise. Whether I had been there or not, the rain would have come; the butterflies would have danced.

But on those days, He paced my steps, so I would witness these splendors of His creation. They were His gifts, to uplift my spirit and remind me He's there.

"Look who I Am. See what I do. I direct the butterflies and time the raindrops. And I hold you."

by Sandra Grace

Psalms 19:1. "The heavens declare the glory of God..."
Hebrews 1:3. "... He (Christ) ... upholds all things by the word of His power ..." (NASB)

Scott's Bay Nova Scotia
Sandra Grace Photography

Scott's Bay Nova Scotia
Sandra Grace Photography

Scott's Bay Nova Scotia
Sandra Grace Photography

Pat Williams Nova Scotia
Sandra Grace Photography

Annapolis Valley
from The Lookoff Nova Scotia
Sandra Grace Photography

Petitcodiac River
Moncton New Brunswick
Sandra Grace Photography

Eclipsed

We sped along highway 515 underneath a glorious sky. After many days of snow, rain, and drab grey, the warm sunshine felt like a wearisome weight had been lifted.

"They've been celebrating all weekend," my mother and co-adventurer told me. Indeed, the hotels were booked solid, and the city's population of just over 18,000 was expected to swell to 60,000 by afternoon.

"Maybe we should have come yesterday," I commented, beginning to fear we might not even get into the city much less find parking or standing room with a view. Vehicles were already lining the highway, and parking lots in various communities we passed were filled with cars and people milling about their telescopes and camera tripods.

After an hour and a half of driving, we reached Miramichi, New Brunswick, the grand theatre for one of the greatest performances we'd ever get to see:

A total solar eclipse.

The crowded sidewalks and heavy traffic I'd expected were, instead, sparse and free flowing. We zipped across Centennial Bridge and headed west along the Miramichi River. I found free parking right on the main drag, and we walked from there down to Ritchie Warf, picking up a pair of protective eyeglasses for each of us from a helpful lady along the way.

We got our first glimpse of the spectacle just moments after the daytime moon began to overtake the sun. Though it was still small scale at that point, it was already impressive. Even more important was the excitement the sight of this heavenly phenomenon sparked within us—anticipation of the greater show to come.

And now, we wait.

When I first read about this event, slated for April 8, 2024, I was at home in Shaunavon, Saskatchewan. How great it would be, I thought, to experience a total solar eclipse! I'd never seen one. Partial eclipses, yes, many times—all very impressive. But this one, a total eclipse, would be something completely set apart from any other.

A total solar eclipse is when the earth, (new) moon, and sun align perfectly, and the moon completely blocks the sun's light, casting the area into brief darkness. A total solar eclipse occurs somewhere on earth about every 18 months. But to be in its path—to get to see one—is rare indeed. The eclipse on April 8 would be happening practically in the backyard of my former residence in New Brunswick! To me, it seemed so close... Yet so very far away—a thing I couldn't quite grasp, now living halfway across the country. The next time one such eclipse will pass over the Maritimes is in 2079. I might not make it for that one.

And yet, through a strange twist of events, here I stand on the banks of the Miramichi River, now directly under the blackening midday sun.

As 4:30 p.m. approaches, the waterfront begins to darken. I go back and forth between watching my surroundings and donning my eclipse glasses to peek at the brilliant crescent as it gets narrower and narrower until now it's just a sliver.

The final point of visible sun gleams, giving a "diamond ring" effect: when sunlight filters through the moon's valleys, mountains, and craters, creating drops of light along the edges of the moon.

4:35 p.m. The sky suddenly becomes like dusk as the black orb completely obscures the sun. Cheers erupt from the crowd as we all stand in wonder. The breeze picks up and shadow bands dance across the ground—truly spectacular! The air cools, but I don't notice a significant difference. Maybe I'm too caught up in what's happening, trying to take in everything at once.

For three minutes and eight seconds we look with the naked eye at the ring of white light that surrounds the perfect circle of the moon like a halo. Stunning!

And then it passes.

The crowd cheers again as the first tiny point of the sun becomes visible and night sky abruptly returns to day. I let go the breath I'm holding.

I wish I could capture what I saw...to share it...to replay it anytime. But some things are too extraordinary to be held...too exceptional to linger, even in a photograph. The true magnificence of those images remains now only in my memory and in the memories of those who saw it with me.

The heavens declare the glory of God. Psalm 19:1

Sandra Grace Photography

Along Route 17, Ontario

The Marvel of His Love

BY SANDRA GRACE

I'm bundled in jacket and blankets, out on the balcony in zero-degree temps. It's Easter morning. The air is clean and crisp with April freshness. This is the last morning I'll be able to see the moon as it wanes. By tomorrow, it will set too far south to view from my perch here. City traffic is sparse but constant. Between the hum of passing cars is a delightful stillness, broken only by the song of ducks and geese on the water below.

Easter. Reflection.

As a kid, I just accepted God's love for me. It was told to me every week in Sunday School. I knew of it like I knew my name. I never thought it through.

Now, I marvel at it. Mystery. Beauty. Undeserved gift. His is a perfect love, a love that cost Him His Son. What a price to pay for the likes of me!

That His love is only one side of the coin makes it that much more incredible. For the other side is His holiness and justice. Sobering. Fearsome. Because He's holy, He cannot excuse sin. Because He's just, He must punish it.

I'm accountable for my wrongs. My sin is a stain I can't wash clean. Somehow that I can't explain, God looked at me and loved me anyway. He sacrificed His Son to pay my debt. Jesus took my punishment for me. When I repented, He cleansed me white as snow. He gave me a new heart. He rescued me. He took me in and made me His own. It was not because of me that He did it. I was nothing. Only He could give me value.

Love balances judgment; they are equally God. It was God's love that chose me and purchased my freedom from His judgment. For His glory.

This is what makes me marvel.

Isaiah 1:18. Though your sins be as scarlet, they will be as white as snow; though they are red like crimson, they will be like wool. (NIV)

Ezekiel 36:26. Moreover, I will give you a new heart and put a new spirit within you; and I will remove the heart of stone from your flesh and give you a heart of flesh. (NASB)

Isaiah 53:3-6. He is despised and rejected of men; a man of sorrows, and acquainted with grief: and we hid as it were our faces from him; he was despised, and we esteemed him not. Surely he hath borne our griefs, and carried our sorrows: yet we did esteem him stricken, smitten of God, and afflicted. But he was wounded for our transgressions, he was bruised for our iniquities: the chastisement of our peace was upon him; and with his stripes we are healed. All we like sheep have gone astray; we have turned every one to his own way; and the Lord hath laid on him the iniquity of us all. (KJV)

01

SONGS OF SPRING

By Sandra Grace

Anyone who's been within earshot of a Nova Scotia pond on a late May evening knows why they are called a *chorus* of frogs. Though these little amphibians may grunt and grumble while lazing in the water in solitude on a warm afternoon, when evening falls and they come together around the shores and among the reeds, they sing. The cool night air fills with sweet notes, sharp and clear: nature's choir, heralding hope and new life—the songs of spring.

It comes with reluctance in the Maritimes, holding back...taunting...maybe shy. Then suddenly, spring breaks through, erupting in full color. Deep scarlet adorns the red maples. There are rose-pink crabapple blossoms, bright yellow forsythia, lilies, blue flags, and purple clusters of lilacs.

02

Enticed by rain showers and the warmth of the sun, new leaves, tender and bright, peek out from their buds. Once satisfied that all is ready, they emerge quickly, as though making up for lost time. They clothe every shrub and tree in shades of rich green, lush and moist. The foliage becomes so thick—bulging—it's as if the forest can't contain its own, and all will burst, any minute, out of its bounds, into the fields and onto the roads.

Deep in the woodlands are more painted treasures: lady slippers; trilliums; lily of the valley; purple violets. And if you can find them, hidden in the cool, damp shadows are delicate blooms of sweetly fragrant mayflowers.

Never far from the woodlands are the beaches, and it's here that time is forgotten. Bask in the sound of ocean waves, breaking on the shores.

03

Hear the squawk of gulls overhead and the flap of a sail in the breeze. Breathe it in: the smell of salt air. Feel the grit between the toes and the warm sun that kisses the face.

Unheedingly, time advances. Too soon, the bright yellow ball sinks, shimmering, into the edge of the earth. Its rays sparkle like diamonds on the dancing ripples; they reach across the water, beckoning.

And there wells up within a longing to stay... To see and hear and dream a little more... On the beaches...in the woodlands...in the fields and on the hills...

Just a little longer in the Maritimes.

01. In Scott's Bay
02. Baxter's Harbor
03. Cape Split
04. Red trillium
05. Apple blossoms
06. Purple violets

REFLECTIONS OF A FATHER

STOCK PHOTO

They fly into my arms the minute I open the door. There are squeals of "Daddy's home!" accompanied by sweet kisses. I sink to the floor and they settle into my lap, recounting all the tales of the kindergarten and third-grade classrooms today. It's a ritual I wouldn't trade for the world.

My wife appears in the hallway, looking a little irritated; but then she blows me a kiss. She tells me about a leak in the upstairs bathroom, and I know how I'll be spending my evening. She leaves us to our talk for a little longer before calling the kids to help in the kitchen.

I remain on the floor, watching them set the table. Something about the tilt of my daughter's head…the light in her eyes…and instantly I'm back to eight years ago…

I'm the worried dad. Things got dicey, and I feared I could lose them both. But suddenly, it's over, and they place the tiny bundle in my arms, healthy and safe. I look into her pinched little face for the first time, and my heart stops for just a moment. It might be that I'm the only one who thinks it—a father's pride—but she's beautiful. I see a hint of me in that determined chin, but mostly, it's my wife I see in our baby girl: in her delicate nose and her long, dark lashes. She takes my breath away.

And I think of all the evils in this world, prowling for the innocent. I tuck my new daughter into me, my shoulders and arms around her like a shield. *Not my little girl. Dear God, please protect this little girl.*

I bring my thoughts back to the present and pull myself up from the floor. I hear the lawnmower sputter and choke, so I go out to see what's wrong. He's there in the backyard, bent over the mower, screwdriver in hand. I can see the intensity on his face. He mutters something to himself. It's only a few minutes before he straightens up, tucks the screwdriver into his belt, and pulls the cord. The mower roars to life, and he resumes his task, unaware of my presence.

Everyone says he looks just like me, my oldest son, this teenager, caught somewhere between *boy* and *man*. I see it in the way he wipes his brow. It's in his walk; his gestures; his crooked grin.

Boys copy their dads, sometimes on purpose; sometimes it's just in the genes. That's how it's supposed to be.

And I'm overcome with the magnitude of this responsibility I carry—to be a man worth copying.

Conversation flows around our dinner table. We all take turns relating our day. The kids tell jokes and stories. I can be a pretty funny guy, and before long, I have everyone in stitches. No one seems in a hurry to wrap it up.

I'm particularly grateful tonight for dinners like this one...for family moments like these. I readily admit it isn't always this way. Our home is not a Hallmark®greeting card—some dinner talks here go from bickering to near brawl. But we work at it.

When we've finished our meal, I pull out the old Bible. I open it up to the place marked with a pressed buttercup taped to a piece of torn paper—my Father's Day gift two years ago.

And it hits me that, to God, my best offerings are just as small and imperfect, yet His pleasure in them is just as big as mine is in this little flower when they're given out of love and obedience to Him. And I wonder, will He turn my feeble efforts as a broken father and husband into something good, so my family doesn't pay the price for my mistakes?

I look up at the faces around the table that are looking back at me, expectantly. They've no idea that my mind is not on the passage in front of me but on them: how precious they are.

How do I do it? How do I lead them into Truth, grounding them, loving and guarding them, listening, teaching my children respect and obedience, treasuring my wife as I do my own life?

The weight of it presses on my chest. It wraps around me, squeezing the breath from my lungs.

My only answer is to fall to my knees. To saturate myself with His Word. To turn my weakness over to Him. *Help me, God, be the father and husband they deserve.*

Twelve little feet patter through our old house. I sit in my chair, trying to stay out of the way as the ladies flutter and fuss over the newest member of our family. My wife is beaming. She recites, again, her latest grandchild's endearing features, and her audience *oohs* and *aahs* in agreement. Her silver hair flows around her face. Her eyes sparkle. She's stunning. But now, I'm distracted. She catches my eye and winks at me, and I wink back.

Chloe, my daughter-in-law, places the little one in my arms, and I get a tingling of déjà vu. He yawns and stretches and settles into me to sleep. Helpless one. So deeply loved.

I thought it would get easier once my children were grown. You know, my job would be done and I could rest. Instead, there are more faces looking up at me; more tender hearts needing guidance; more innocence to guard.

My son takes the seat beside me. "Sometimes, I just stare at him," he tells me, nodding toward the baby. "He's so small. It sucks the air right out of me. Ever feel like that, Dad? Like, how are you ever going to do it?"

"Every single day, Son."

"Grampa, come chase us," little voices call. "Come play with us, Grampa."

"Outside!" Four women shout in unison.

I pass the baby to his father and head for the door. "Come on, kids." There's a raucous of hoorays and laughter and pounding shoes on the hardwood floor.

The job is never over, not till a man breathes his last breath. My family is mine for as long as I'm here, and the responsibility only grows with time. They are God's, entrusted to me, a treasure and blessing. It's a sobering truth: my accountability for how I handle God's calling on me to care for them, to protect and lead them.

I gird myself in His armor and trust Him for the battle against the evils that threaten from without and within. And I know He is faithful.

I rest my hands on two tiny heads. *God, keep these little ones.*

by Sandra Grace

Sainte-Hélène-de-Bagot, Quebec
Sandra Grace Photography

Saint-Basile, New Brunswick
Sandra Grace Photography

The Addiction

It began innocently enough. *"Go ahead. Try it. It'll be good, you'll see."*

No one mentioned the hold it would have on me, that it would infiltrate almost every part of my life. Just one more...

So once again I sling my camera over my shoulder and hit the road, searching for subjects to capture with my lens. Among my favorites are old buildings—ancient churches, weathered houses, collapsing barns—and the panoramas of these beautiful Canadian provinces.

Every turn in the road offers another view. Every abandoned old farmhouse whispers of the past—a family; a story. I can get lost in the magic. No matter how many times I click the shutter, there's always one more angle, one more shot.

In the spring of 2022, I embarked on one of my most exciting adventures—a six-day drive from Saskatchewan to Nova Scotia and back. Along the way, I met some of the loveliest people, and at my destination, I enjoyed the company of treasured family and friends. Many of the photos featured in this book were taken on that trip.

~ Sandra Grace

Secret of Amethyst Cove

by Sandra Grace

   We packed up early Saturday morning and drove to Cape Split Park, Nova Scotia. Strapping on backpacks that contained snacks, bottled water, and extra clothing, we started off on a trail that would take us uphill for the next kilometer-and-a-half.

   "The shore is rocky," my son explained. "So it's hard going. And we need to get out before the tide comes in. But first," he warned, "we have to climb down a 400-foot cliff just to get to the beach. Are you okay with that?"

   "I'm not sure..." I hesitated. "I'll let you know when we get there." *Why do there always have to be cliffs?*

   But this was Amethyst Cove—our destination; our reward. Mystery. Intrigue. Pirates and treasure came to mind. Of course, its secrets would be uncovered only by first conquering formidable foes like cliffs and rocks and rushing tides.

   Our path led us through the woods. Blue sky peeked out from an expanse of white, fluffy clouds. The ground was soggy after days of rain, and I had to leave the trail several times, skirting stretches of mud and water, to avoid soaking the only footwear I'd brought with me for the weekend.

At last, we came to the top of the crag that looked out at the Bay of Fundy. From that height, the shore below appeared like sand and the water, smooth. My, how perspective can distort the truth.

Beside us, long ropes, tightly knotted around thick tree trunks, snaked down from the edge. We grabbed hold and started our descent. The first 80 feet or so were a manageable slope. This wasn't so bad.

My son and his two boys scrambled down ahead of me and waited at a small outcropping. As I drew closer, I noticed the bluff beyond them seemed to drop straight away. *That's it. I'm done.* And I was already planning how to pass the time there alone while they continued without me.

As I reached the spot, all three of them disappeared into the abyss. I peered over the side to see their smiling faces among the rocks. Relief washed over me. Though this section was much steeper, there were good toe holds all the way to where the slope became gentler again.

And I knew then that I would not turn back.

We hit the beach just after 10:15 a.m. low tide. My son pointed to a jut of land down the coast. "On the other side is Amethyst Cove," he said.

"That's a long way. Do we have time to get there and back?"

"If it were just the two of us, yes." He shrugged, "I'm not sure, though, with the kids."

"Then we best get going."

We set off, stumbling over stones and picking our way through boulders that had tumbled to the beach in a landslide. The kids scoured the ground for interesting rocks, packing their pockets with their favorites. I admit, my hurry soon waned as I, too, searched for nuggets of amethyst, fabled to have been cast throughout the menacing terrain.

Wispy fog seeped over the shore ahead of us, and the farther we went into the mist, the colder and windier it got. We tired quickly; we sat on boulders to rest and munch on apples and steak slices.

By the time we resumed our quest, my younger grandson had had enough. He wanted to go back. We prodded him along for a while, but we knew the climb out would be much more taxing on all of us if he were to overdo it down here.

I gazed at the point of land way in the distance. "We aren't going to make it, are we?"

Time was running out and tide waits for no man.

We turned around and headed back toward the trail, leading up from the beach.

No, we never got to see Amethyst Cove or learn its secrets. But what a glorious day just the same.

For the prize wasn't the cove or its gems. The real treasure was the adventure itself—conquering the cliff...racing against the tide...

And that we did it together.

SON OF THE FATHER

In a dank, dark prison cell stands a man condemned to die. His hands on the cold stone wall, he looks up at the narrow shaft of light from the only window high above his head. Outside is commotion—the crowd growing ever larger and louder. They're angry and shouting. What's happening? He stretches upward, but there's no way to see; no way to reach the small opening.

He turns from the wall and resumes his pacing. How much longer till they come for him? His heartbeat quickens despite his resolve. He's lived a vile life. He's a thief, a terrorist, a murderer. Now, he stares death in the face—execution, as he deserves. Long, slow torture. He clenches his jaw, his face, set.

STOCK PHOTO

Footsteps clop on the stones in the corridor, closer and closer to his cell. Metal jangles with each step—keys that hang from the guard's belt. The lock clangs and the door opens. "Come on, come on," the guard grabs him roughly and shoves him into the narrow passageway. From beyond the walls, he hears the throng, "Crucify him! Crucify him!" they shout. The chant rings louder as he stumbles up the steps into the bright courtyard.

But instead of being led away with the other prisoners, he's brought before Pilate. The Roman governor reads out his release and stamps it with his seal. And the condemned man is pardoned. Pilate glances down at him, a look like stone, then whisks away. Barabbas stares after the governor, unable to move. It has to be a mistake. No one would pardon him.

"You're free," the guard tells him and nudges him back down the steps from the portico. He nods toward the road that leads out of the city. "They're taking Him instead."

Barabbas cranes his neck and peers through the crowd. A man, beaten and bloody, stumbles under the weight of a heavy cross. "Who is He?" he asks.

"Jesus of Nazareth. He says He's the king of the Jews," the guard snickers. "The king who will die in your place."

"The king who takes my place ..." Barabbas repeats slowly, tasting each word. "Jesus will die, and I'll go free."

* * *

Thursday morning, March 5, 2020, I stood in the empty tomb in Jerusalem. They were sobering moments as I gazed on the place where, possibly, the Son of God had lain. It's not known if this is the actual tomb of Christ, and there are arguments for and against it. But whether or not it's the one, I know His grave is empty.

Garden Tomb, Jerusalem
Photo by Sandra Grace

From the tomb, our group gathered in a garden alcove, a communion tray on the marble table before us—precious moments of reflection together on the sacrifice freely offered for us. The gift of God's pardon and eternal life to those who trust and repent.

It was our group leader who pointed out the connection between Barabbas and us (me):

Jerusalem
Sandra Grace Photography

'Bar' in Aramaic means 'son;'
'Abbas' means 'father.'
—Son of the father.

I am Barabbas.
I am the guilty one set free. Jesus of Nazareth—God, innocent One—took my place so that I could become a son (daughter) of the Father.

Hallelujah! What a Savior!

by Sandra Grace

20

MOTHER

The young mothers are gathered in my kitchen, cooing over babies and kissing owies on toddlers. They laugh together at the antics of their little ones, radiating with pleasure in their children.

What a beautiful place they hold, those who are mothers, to be charged with the training and shaping of miniature people who are the future of our world. What an honor to be trusted with these tender hearts and lives.

A mother's love. It begins with her first awareness of her babies' existence, and it binds them as sure as the umbilical cord. She dreams of their little faces, their fingers and toes. She carries them close to her heart while they are being knit together by the hands of the Creator. They are one with her yet uniquely individual.

At last, their anticipated arrival. Her pain in their birth is quickly forgotten when she hears their first cries and cuddles them to her. She rejoices in the new life.

Her nights are sleepless, tending to sickness and cries of hunger and bad dreams. Her days are filled with feeding, washing, nursing cuts, stitching dresses for dolls, building forts, plucking pebbles out of noses, comforting broken hearts, cleaning up after, and putting to bed. The load is heavy. She's exhausted and sometimes discouraged. Yet she wouldn't trade it for anything.

Her children are her richest blessing, her greatest pride. She heralds their accomplishments and swells with joy as they shine. They are her deepest heartache and biggest worry. Has she taught them well? Will they remember to do what's right? Are they in danger—their bodies...their souls? She covers them with her prayers and commits them to God.

She puts on them responsibility and holds them accountable, so they will learn that life is work. She teaches them to give and to consider others because their lives must be about more than themselves. She corrects and disciplines. She demands their obedience and respect. She doesn't give in when they resent her, for she knows the character she's building in them is of far greater worth than having their favor now.

And she watches them grow. The toddler pushes into childhood; childhood surges into adolescence. Her boy and her girl begin to fade, and the man and woman they will become begin to take shape before her. Adolescence transforms into adulthood. And all too soon, she lets them go.

She is all of this. She is Mother. What a beautiful word. *Her children rise up and call her blessed.*

Amidst the commotion and laughter in my kitchen, I think about my own mother—the one who gave me life, who taught me and raised me; the one who showed me what it is to be a mother. I tried to live up to her example when I had children of my own. I soon learned the enormity of the task, the joys and sorrows, and what it is to watch the years fly by.

Now I'm the grandmother. The moms and dads who surround me are my children, and it's their children who fill my house today. It's a double celebration: Mother's Day and the birth of our newest grandbaby. We all marvel again at his full head of hair. We take his hands from inside the blanket and look at his fingers; we inspect his toes. Satisfied that all ten digits are just as cute as they were when we checked fifteen minutes ago, Chloe takes him to the living room and places him into his grandfather's arms. I look over at my husband who seems a little lost in the wonder of the tiny bundle he's holding. At last, he looks up at me. I wink, and he winks back.

"Grampa, come play with us," the kids all shout, crowding around him.

"Outside!" we women call at once. With a kiss on the tiny forehead, Grampa hands over baby to its father, then he and the children stampede for the door. With a slam, all goes quiet at last, and the house seems to sigh with relief.

I look at the faces of the women in my kitchen, and we all giggle. Through the window, I see my husband marching across the backyard with a trail of kids behind him like the Pied Piper. My son is somewhere down the hall, singing softly to his new boy—the sweetest sound in the world.

My family: the very air I breathe and the beat of my heart. They are etched into my soul, forever a part of me.

Because I'm their mother.

by Sandra Grace
Psalm 139:13-16. Proverbs 31:28.

Photograph

Sandra Grace Photography

I SPUN AROUND IN TIME TO SEE A KID DISAPPEAR INTO ONE OF THE HOUSES. MAYBE THIS PLACE WASN'T ABANDONED AFTER ALL.

Strewn across the Saskatchewan prairie are countless old abandoned buildings in various stages of decay. Their weathered exteriors with dark window holes incite the imagination to mystery and rumination. Photographers are drawn to their forlorn majesty, tramping through overgrown hedges and muck to get just the right angle for their shots. I never saw the appeal.

At dawn today, I was zipping along Highway 13, pleased with myself for having gotten on the road so early. There was no traffic, so I was making good time. I found an oldies station on the radio, and I piped in with my vocals as backup. All was well till my car gave a cough and a sputter, and it chugged to a stop at the side of the highway. Now what? I pulled out my cell phone, hoping it had just enough juice left to make one call, but I already knew it was dead. And I'd left the charger back home on the kitchen counter.

I grabbed my jacket—because March is chilly in Saskatchewan—and my brand-new camera—because my wife had insisted I needed a hobby—and I walked a kilometer and a half in the frigid morning till I saw what looked like a house down a side road. There was nothing else in sight. So I headed toward it.

What I found was a ghost town. A whole hamlet of collapsing sheds and houses and barns and fields littered with ancient, rusting machinery. Looking up and down the empty street, I saw not a sign of life anywhere. Serves me right for taking a shortcut. I turned and stared back the way I'd come. How much farther would I walk before reaching civilization?

I'd just set off when there came the sound of a door opening somewhere behind me. I spun around in time to see a kid disappear into one of the houses. Maybe this place wasn't abandoned after all. "Hey!" I called, breaking into a jog. "I need to use your phone."

At the step, I paused. Not a sound. The door swung inward at my knock, revealing a kitchen to my right, a hallway ahead, and dining and living rooms to the left. All were in shambles. Cupboard doors hung off the hinges; there were broken dishes on the floor; the barrel of an old ringer washer lay on its side in the corner. Bird and rodent droppings caked every surface. This place had not seen human occupation in a long time.

Which made me wonder where that kid had gone. The heavy layer of dirt on the floor was undisturbed—not a footprint anywhere.

I should have minded my business, but curiosity got the better of me. I stepped slowly across the disaster zone of a kitchen, through the dining room, and into the living room. Or was it a parlor...? And what was the difference, anyway?

At the staircase, I reached for the banister, then abruptly drew back. *Don't touch it, Jack! Disease-ridden, vermin-infested place.*

I tested the first step, easing onto it. It creaked, like old houses do, but it held. By the third step, I was feeling more confident. The fourth one was half missing, so I skipped it and went to the fifth.

Coming onto the sixth step, I got my first glimpse of the upper level. The old place must have had some sort of mysterious power because I was actually feeling intrigued. There was some fine workmanship here. The detail in the trim on the...

Whoosh! Out of nowhere, came an assault of squawks and flutters, scaring me out of my skin, and a squadron of psychotic birds dive-bombed my head. Instinctively, I crouched and threw up my hands. It took only that sudden shift of my weight to bring a sickening sound of splintering wood, and the step gave way under me. I lunged for the banister that I'd so carefully avoided just thirty seconds before—it was all that saved my hide from landing in the basement.

I managed to pull my foot out of the hole. I'd banged up my shin pretty good, and blood had already soaked through my pant leg. My attackers were, by now, nowhere to be seen, having raced off to torment some other poor sod, no doubt. I don't know what made me keep going, but once I'd found a somewhat reliable tread, I continued my climb, hugging the wall and squinting intently into the dim light in case there were more Kamikazes lurking in the rafters.

The second story had four large bedrooms. I peered into each one, but there was nothing of note but broken, wrought iron bed frames and miscellaneous debris.

In the master bedroom, I stood at the window, staring out at the yard. It was brown and drab, adorned with dead grass, bare twigs, and mud. I wondered if even springtime could rescue it.

Turning to leave, I noticed the desk on the opposite wall. It was a fine piece of furniture and still in surprisingly good condition. I opened it up and rummaged through the cubbyholes along the back. There were a few odds and ends, but mostly, it was empty.

Then something caught my eye—a slip of paper wedged between a divider and the desk frame. I used my pocketknife to get hold of it and eased it out of its hiding place.

It was a letter.

January 28, 1918. My darling, Thomas, it began.

I cannot put into words how much I miss you, my Love. Your gentle hand ... your warm kiss ... especially now with the winter so cold and the nights so long ...

Goodness! I set the paper back on the desk. A love letter! Intimate secrets of the heart! I scratched at the back of my neck as heat rose from under my collar. "You're a snoop, Jack," I chided myself and turned away.

"Why, yes, in fact, I am," I responded, smugly, going back to pick up the letter again.

It has been particularly difficult since my mother's passing. You know what a friend she was to me and a help with the children. Papa still checks in on us every week and brings us wood for the stove. Last week, he repaired the handle on that old axe. He is such a dear. He asks after you every time, and I think he misses you almost as much as I do. Of course, he misses Mama terribly.

Well, I knew a bit about that, didn't I?

Papa says Winston is the spitting image of you. You know, he's right. These last few months, our boy suddenly bears a striking resemblance to his papa, in both looks and manner. How it thrills me to see your son growing so strong and good, becoming so much like you.

When will you be home, my husband? It's more than five weeks since I've heard from you. What has happened? I long for just a word to reassure my frightened heart...to know that you are okay.

I must tell you a funny story, Darling. You know how the children sometimes squabble. Yesterday, while I was making bread, the twins got up to some mischief. Well, right away, Alex toddled over to...

Alex toddled over to what? The rest of the page was empty. I flipped the letter over, but the back was blank too. Why hadn't she finished it? I needed more. I had to know about this young wife and mother who had held her family together in Nowhere, Saskatchewan in the frigid winter of 1918. I ripped open the desk drawers one by one. All were empty.

Then I noticed the space inside the bottom drawer was shorter than the others. About four inches shorter. I felt around—tapped, pushed, pulled—and finally something let go, and the back of the drawer slid out, revealing a small compartment. *Well, well. What have we here?* Tattered and yellowed documents, a few photos, and a whole bundle of letters. I pulled out the first.

March 1, 1917. Sweet Suzanna,

I'm thrilled at how happy you are with the house. It was only with your Papa's help that I was able to have it ready for you before I left. I'm thankful for those few weeks you and I spent in it together.

I heard from Zeke the other day. He says a family moved into the house on the corner. Have you met them? Perhaps the children will make new friends. He tells me, too, there is talk of a shop going up on Bradley Street this spring. I know you will like that, Sweetheart. Our little town is booming.

I do so enjoy your stories of the children. That little Alex! What an adorable rascal! How I ache to meet him.

You asked what it is like for me here. My Darling, I will not frighten you with talk of war. I will only say, this is the most horrible place I have ever seen. Death and suffering are so ugly, no matter on what side we fight. But I am safe and well, and I pray to God that He brings me back quickly to you and our family.

I do miss you, Suz, and can hardly wait to hold you again.

All my love, Thomas

And there were more, many more...

An hour and a half later, I was sprawled on the floor, empty envelopes scattered around me. I looked at the photos in my hand, presumably of Suzanna and Thomas. I'd learned that Suzanna Phillips Kennedy was 24 years old when she wrote that letter in January of 1918. Thomas Kennedy was 30 and an army captain, stationed in France. Before that, he'd been a veterinarian. They had moved to this town in 1915, and Thomas had built this house for Suzanna and their three children: Winston and the twins, Sarah and Gwendolyn. Alexander had come along just nine months after Thomas had left for Europe. Interesting.

This town had been something back then. The CP rail line went through on its way to Stirling. There were grain elevators on the outskirts; shops downtown; a school; a surgeon; even its own hospital. Impressive. People were flocking into the little metropolis that glinted with the promise of prosperity and a bright future.

I went to the window again, and this time I saw something different. The streets were full; the town was alive. The houses were new and freshly painted. People were coming and going at the shops, their footsteps sounding on the wooden sidewalks. Grain dust floated around the elevators. Down on the corner, men sat in the shade, swapping stories of the "good 'ol days." And somewhere below me, the Kennedy children played, their laughter echoing through the hallways of this great house.

You would have loved this, my Becky, I muttered, turning from the window to admire the old bedroom again. That's when I remembered my camera.

I gathered the letters and photos and stuffed them into my pocket. I snapped pictures of the bedroom and the desk; of the kitchen with its broken dishes; of the cookstove and the cupboards. I did closeups of the mantle on the fireplace and of the spindles on the staircase—how had I not noticed before how beautiful the banister was?

I went outdoors and walked the perimeter, examining the time-battered building from every side. This would have been a grand home in 1915. No wonder Suzanna was so happy here. I paused in awe as the past enveloped me.

I raised my camera again. Through my lens I saw them, framed by the open dining room window: pretty Suzanna with little Alex on her hip, setting dishes on the table and calling to the other children; Thomas, taking his seat as everyone gathered round; all of them joining hands while he asks the blessing on the meal... A young family in love with each other. I snapped the shutter, preserving the past forever in my photograph.

Their voices faded as I looked up over my camera at the empty room beyond the missing window pane. Their faces vanished like whips on the wind. What had happened to them? The children? Suzanna? What had prevented her from finishing the letter? Did Thomas make it home from the war?

"Can I help you?" The voice startled me out of my reverie.

"Uh ... yeah. Maybe." I stepped toward the pickup that was idling in the gravel street. "My car broke down out on the highway, and my phone's dead."

"Not your lucky day." The old man handed me his cell through his truck window.

"Oh, I... I don't know about that," I replied, glancing back at the house. I made a couple of calls and soon had a tow truck on its way.

"Need a ride somewhere?" the stranger asked.

"No, thanks. I think I'll wait here."

"Suit yourself," and he started away.

"Just a second," I called after him. "Did you see a kid around here? About ten years old? Yellow jacket?"

"Hasn't been a kid in this town in twenty years."

Twenty years? "But there was a kid here a couple hours ago," I insisted. "I saw him, going into that..."

"That what you saw?" the stranger nodded toward the house.

I looked behind me. Through the open window, a yellow curtain flapped in a gust of wind, and a loose board clapped against the frame. Was that the door I'd heard? I squinted, trying to match the movement of the curtain with what I'd seen earlier. No? Yes? The kid who'd drawn me back into this town just as I was leaving; who'd enticed me into the old mansion; who'd unwittingly introduced me to Thomas and Suzanna... My hand absently went to the packet of letters inside my jacket.

"Maybe..." I muttered. But I wasn't convinced. If this old ghost town could bring to life for me today a family and a community from a century ago... draw me into its breath and its heartbeat, it would have no problem bringing to life one kid in a yellow jacket from 1998. I grinned to myself as the old man drove off.

* * *

It's late when I pull into the driveway—I was supposed to get in hours ago. The sun's going down and the shadows are long across the yard. An old red barn sits at the back corner of the property. The kids are outside, playing with the dog. The little one's clad in only a diaper, his shirt and pants peeled off the instant he was out of sight of his mother, no doubt. Good thing it's warmer here now than where I was this morning.

I step out of the car. My son appears from inside the barn; my daughter-in-law comes from the house. "Kids! Granddad's here!" she calls.

Hugs and kisses all around, and I pull out presents for everyone right there in the yard. Little Ollie wraps himself around my leg, "You took a long time to come back, Granddad."

"A little too long," my son reminds me, and I nod, guiltily. "Have you thought about it?" he asks. "...About staying?"

"How long ya gonna stay, Granddad?" Arthur tugs at my sleeve.

I pick up Ollie and put him on my shoulders. "Well, little buddy, I just might stay the whole summer."

"All summer!" There are cheers from the kids and smiles from my son and daughter-in-law as we head for the door en masse.

And for the second time today, I step into a creaky, old house that echoes with laughter.

SANDRA GRACE

Sandra Grace was born and raised in Moncton, New Brunswick. In 2012, she relocated to the prairies of Saskatchewan and Alberta.

Sandra's passion for writing began at the age of eight, inspired by the encouragement of her third-grade teacher.

She discovered her love of photography around her pond in Airdrie, AB and through her exploration of Alberta and Saskatchewan.

In 2020, Sandra spent two months in Costa Rica working on her memoir, *Wings in the Storm: Hope & Healing through Brokenness*, published in 2021. She is the author of four children's books, under the name, Sandra Fram.

Sandra lives in Shaunavon, Saskatchewan. She works as an administrator and enjoys motorbiking, hiking, photography, travel, family & friends, and of course, writing.

BOOKS

Wings in the Storm; Hope & Healing through Brokenness

Prairie Blossoms Winter

CHILDREN'S BOOKS

The Secrets of Amethyst Cove

Runaway Teeth

Happy Birthday, Mrs. Gimbal

Priscilla's Leaves
   co-authored with her
   daughter, Grace

CONTACT HER

sgracewrites@outlook.com

facebook.com/sandra.grace. 10048379

WEBSITE

wingsinthestorm.ca

"Reflections of a Father," "Mother," & "Photograph" are fiction.

All other stories in *Blossoms* are based on real events.

www.ingramcontent.com/pod-product-compliance
Lightning Source LLC
Chambersburg PA
CBHW041546240626
47164CB00003B/149